T0365616

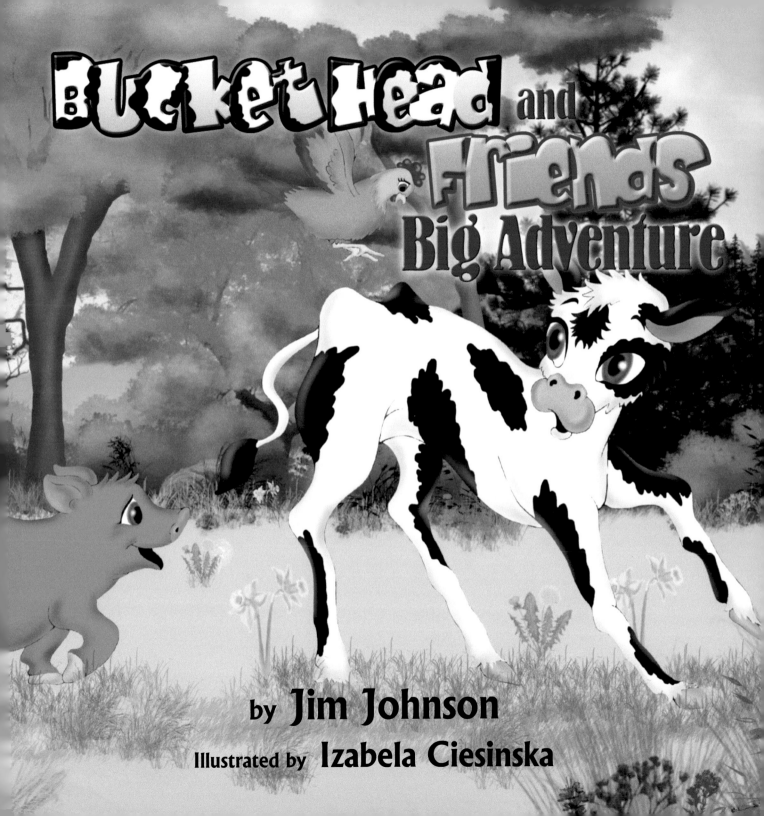

Bucket Head and Friends Big Adventure

by Jim Johnson

Illustrated by Izabela Ciesinska

To order additional copies of this book, contact:
Xlibris
844-714-8691
www.Xlibris.com
Orders@Xlibris.com

Layout Designer: Charito Sim

ISBN: 978-1-4257-9564-1 (sc)
ISBN: 978-1-4771-7514-9 (e)

Print information available on the last page

Rev. date: 01/09/2023

DEDICATED TO MY FAMILY—Mother, Angie Mae Johnson-DuBoise, Sisters— Helen, Barbara, Jackie, Brenda (Tida), Brothers-Grover, Prentis, Green Lee, Anthony, and their families, and all my nieces and nephews. I love you all!

ACKNOWLEDGMENTS—John A Sommer, Thank You for the farm. You are a true friend and will always be a part of my family. You get a free copy of this book autographed! A.J., Sam and Otto!

SPECIAL ACKNOWLEDGMENTS— Linda, Shannon, and Rachel, may all your adventures in life be good. Thank you. Izabela Ciesinska—What can I say. Your illustrations are wonderfull and made this book come alive! You are awesome! You are fun to work with and you will be called upon to do my next adventure! Thank You very much for doing this project!— Izzi E-mail address is izabelaciesinska@hotmail.com— The Spence family, Phil and Maryann,—The Lodjic family, Mike and Elizabeth, Early Head Start—Jo, Bernie, Jaymie, Pat, Diane, Wendy, Gig Harbor Wa.—The Evergreen State College—Tacoma Wa., Brennor and Sue Beck—and, many more! A percentage of sales of this book will go to Children charities!

A farmer, named John, lives on a 155 acre farm he inherited from his grandfather just outside the small town of Pinetop. Everyone calls him "Farmer John" because he is devoted to his farm.

Farmer John has lots of animals; cows, pigs, horses, chickens, a dog named Blitz and a goat named Billy. All the animals love Farmer John because he takes good care of them, rain or shine. He feeds them twice a day and makes sure they have plenty of clean, fresh water.

Farmer John's animals seem like ordinary farm animals, but they aren't. Some of his animals have a big secret. They can talk to each other. No one knows they can talk, because they only talk when no one is around!

Bucket Head is a young calf. He got his name because he gets his head stuck in his feed bucket at feeding time. He just wants to find out what's on the bottom of his bucket. Every day, Farmer John pries his feed bucket from his face.

Poor Bucket Head is filled with curiosity! His friends, Pee Wee the pig and Miss Banty Hen Hen get into so much mischief with Bucket Head.

One day the gate was open when Farmer John was inside his house. Ol' Bucket Head decides it's time to see what's on the other side of the farm! He finds Pee Wee and Miss Banty Hen Hen and tells them his idea. They think it's great! Let's go on an adventure!

Pee Wee is scrambling to keep up the pace, as they leave the barn. "Don't walk so fast Bucket Head. Your legs are longer then mine. I can't keep up!"

Bucket Head replies, "I'm sorry. I'll walk slower. Miss Banty Hen Hen, would you like to ride on my shoulder?"

Miss Banty Hen Hen flaps her wings with excitement and flies up on Bucket Head's shoulders. Slowly, the odd animal trio walk out of the gate, adventuring into the unknown wilds of the farm.

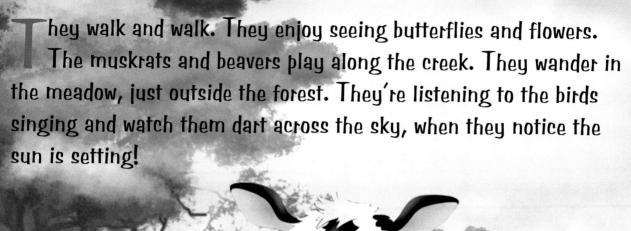

They walk and walk. They enjoy seeing butterflies and flowers. The muskrats and beavers play along the creek. They wander in the meadow, just outside the forest. They're listening to the birds singing and watch them dart across the sky, when they notice the sun is setting!

"Oh, no," said Bucket Head. "I'm getting hungry! Maybe we should get back to the farm before Farmer John notices we are gone."

Pee Wee and Miss Banty Hen Hen exclaim in unison, "I'm getting hungry, too!"

They are all having such a good time, but they don't want Farmer John to worry about them, so they start walking back to the farm.

They walk and walk for a long time. They can't find their way back to the farm. They were so excited and having such a great time, that they forgot which way they came. They look at each other and realize that they are lost.

Pee Wee and Miss Banty Hen Hen look at Bucket Head and say, "What do we do now, Bucket Head?"

Bucket Head replies, "Don't worry. I can find the farm."

Bucket Head looks around, but he doesn't know which way to go. "Let's go this way," he said. "Maybe we can find our old trail." So they did. They walk for a long, long time. They still can't find the trail, or the way back. Now it's really getting dark.

Miss Banty Hen Hen and Pee Wee were really worried now. They are hungry and tired. Pee Wee asks Bucket Head, "What if we never get back? Farmer John will miss us a lot!"

Bucket Head replies, "Don't worry Pee Wee. We'll get back. I promise."

Pee Wee sits on his hind legs, looking all around. I know, he says, I will try to smell for our tracks the way we came . . . and he started rooting.

Pee Wee keeps his nose to the ground. Sniff, sniff Sniff, sniff, sniff! "I think I found something," Pee Wee exclaims, his nose in a hole in the ground.

"What did you find?" Asks Bucket Head, as Pee Wee backs up away from the hole.

"I don't know," says Pee Wee.

Quietly a sleepy, groggy little critter crawls out of her hole. "Do you know which way to go to get back to Farmer John's house?" asks Pee Wee.

Le Belle says, "No . . ." as she comes up to him nose — to — nose. When she realizes how Big Pee Wee is, she starts, turns and lifts her tail straight into the air.

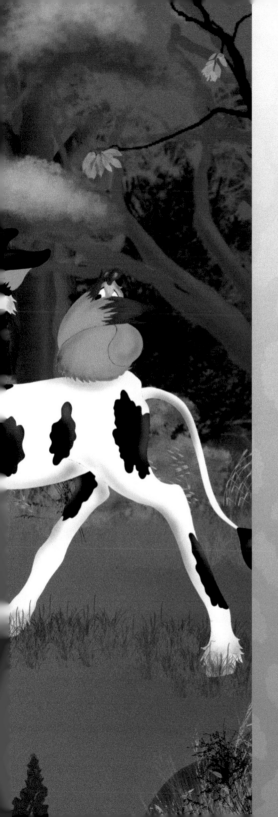

Pee Wee says, "You don't have to be that way! We're just lost and want to go home."

La Belle shakes her fanny. Suddenly Pee Wee squeals! "Help! Help!!! HELP ME!!! Oh, this stinks!" His eyes are watering, his body is shaking. Now, Pee Wee doesn't know what to do.

Bucket Head comes beside him. "Oh, no!!! A Skunk!"

Miss Banty Hen Hen squaks, "The creek! Go to the creek."

They all scramble to the creek. Pee Wee waddles into the creek to wash the smell off.

"What did I do, Bucket Head? I just wanted to be friends!" says Pee Wee.

"You didn't do anything wrong. Some animals aren't friendly like we are, I guess," said Bucket Head.

"No, not everybody's nice," said Miss Banty Hen Hen.

Just as they sit down to rest Miss Banty Hen Hen hears a strange noise calling from the forest.

"What is that?" Miss Banty Hen Hen asks.

"What is what?" Bucket Head and Pee Wee ask.

"THAT!" Miss Banty Hen Hen exclaims.

Bucket Head and Pee Wee hear a sound. "What IS that?" They say together.

"Where did it come from?" asked Bucket Head.

"It came from over there by the edge of the forest" says Pee Wee. "It sounds like someone is calling . . . ."

All three listen intently. They hear someone calling their names! Suddenly Farmer John and his dog, Blitz, come out of the forest!

"It's Farmer John and Blitz" they all scream together! "They came to take us home!"

"Someone tangled with a skunk!" exclaimed Farmer John, with a chuckle. "Huh? Suppose you'd like to tell me about it?" he asked with a twinkle in his eye.

They all speak up at once. Squeals, moos and clucks. Farmer John doesn't understand a single sound. He smiles, knowing they're glad to see him!

They are so excited, they run to Farmer John. Bucket Head licks John's face with his tongue. Farmer John says, "I'm going to get you a cow bell to put around your neck, so this doesn't happen again!"

At first Pee Wee is running in circles like a pig trying to catch his curly tail! Finally, he runs up to Farmer John and starts rooting by his foot, while Miss Banty Hen Hen flaps her wings and clucks.

They are so happy they can't contain their excitement and start singing, "Merry, Merry, Merry We, We're as happy as can be." Farmer John didn't know what they were singing.

"We're going HOME!" said Pee Wee. "To eat and see our other friends on the farm."

"We need to get you three ready for the county fair next week." Farmer John says.

All three squeal with excitement!

"Maybe we can explore the fair!" Bucket Head exclaims.

"Yes!!" said Pee Wee and Miss Banty Hen Hen. "We can hardly wait to explore the fair!!"

Printed in the United States
by Baker & Taylor Publisher Services